Mary Bahr

The Memory Box

Illustrated by *David Cunningham*

ALBERT WHITMAN & COMPANY
Chicago, Illinois

For my grandparents, who made memories for me,

And for my parents, who make memories for my sons.—M.B.

Library of Congress Cataloging-in Publication Data

Bahr, Mary
The memory box / Mary Bahr;
Illustrated by David Cunningham.
p. cm.
Summary: When Gramps realizes he has Alzheimer's disease, he starts a memory box
with his grandson, Zach, to keep memories of all the times they have shared.

[1. Grandfathers—Fiction. 2. Alzheimer's disease—Fiction.]
PZ7.B1434Me 1992   91-21628
[E]—dc20   CIP
                                                            AC

Text copyright © 1992 by Mary Bahr.
Illustrations copyright © 1992 by David Cunningham.
Published in 1992 by Albert Whitman & Company
ISBN 978-0-8075-5053-3

Printed in China
15 14 13 12 11 10 NP 20 19 18 17 16 15

Designed by Karen Johnson Campbell.
The illustrations are gouache.
The text typeface is ITC Stone Informal.

For more information about Albert Whitman & Company,
visit our web site at www.albertwhitman.com.

My thanks to Flo Carris, Coordinator of the Colorado Springs Alzheimer Steering Committee, and Moira Reinhardt, Administrator of Namaste Alzheimer Center, dedicated caregivers who read this manuscript and said, "Yes, this is the way it is." To Kathy Tucker, a special first editor. And to my husband, Bill Fritts, and our four sons, Jason, Joshua, Jordan, and Jeremy, whose patience with many make-your-own-sandwich nights gave me the time to make my own story.—M.B.

When I woke up this morning, I knew it was going to be a great vacation. Gramps was standing by my bed, holding the tackle box.

"Already too hot for catching walleye," he said.

"I bet Zach would like to throw out a line anyway, this being his first day," Gram argued from the doorway. She was holding a plateful of butter-dripping cinnamon rolls. As I said, it was going to be a great vacation. Three weeks of fishing on Gramps's lake and eating Gram's cooking.

Now, from the boat, I could see Gram waving at us fishermen from the dock on the sky blue lake. Behind her on the hillside sat their berry red house in the middle of the dark green northern woods. The color reminded me of a painting I saw once.

Gramps and I rested our bamboo poles on the side of the boat. Our bobbers rode the glittery waves.

"It's a Memory Box day," Gramps said as we waited for the perch to decide if they were hungry.

"What's a Memory Box?" I asked, dangling my hands in the cool water. I wondered if fish ever nibbled fingers.

"Remind me to tell you after the fish fry we're gonna have tonight. Now let's get quiet and catch 'em."

And we did. We got so quiet I could hear the fish circling our night crawlers. But it still took three hours of sweaty, itchy stillness before we hauled in enough to fill Gram's skillet.

"Don't forget the Cook's Rule," Gram said as we unloaded our catch. We always cleaned ourselves and the fish in the lakeside shed. But every summer Gram reminded us, anyway! "Nothing but good smells at my dinner table," she'd say, pushing us back out if we tried to sneak in without washing first.

In the shed, for the first time ever, Gramps handed me the long filet knife, the knife that's about a hundred years old. The one I hope will be mine someday.

"I think you're old enough to handle the blade," he said, "and to hear the true tale of the Cook's Rule." He guided my fingers as I gutted my fish. "That first time I caught fish for Gram to cook, I brought them into the kitchen to clean. I don't think she was prepared for fish eyes staring back at her out of the sink. She screamed so loud I dropped the frypan and broke my toe. After that, the fish and I went to the shed."

We laughed. Everybody knew Gramps usually made up most of his "true tales."

After dinner, we dragged our fish-full bellies to the porch to watch the sun slip into the lake. Crickets fiddled and owls hoo-ooted, but the rest of the world was quiet. All except Gram and Gramps and me in our rickety rockers on the wooden porch.

"Hmm-mmmm-m." Gramps was settling in, getting ready for another true tale. He's a great storyteller. Gram thinks so, I know, because she always puts down her cross-stich when he begins.

"It was your Great-Gram who told me about the Memory Box," Gramps said, staring at the sunset sky. "It's a special box that stores family tales and traditions. An old person and a young person fill the box together. Then they store it in a place of honor. No matter what happens to the old person, the memories are saved forever."

"What do you mean, 'no matter what happens'?" I asked Gramps. I didn't like his story much.

The sun practically disappeared before Gramps answered. "Do you know this old body just flunked a physical exam for the first time?"

Gram stopped rocking.

"This old person must make his Memory Box," Gramps said after a long silence. He stopped rocking, too, and looked me square in the eye. "Is this young person ready?"

"I guess. Sure." The words stuck in my mouth like caramel from a Halloween apple.

Gram disappeared into the house and made a pots-and-pans racket.

"Zach? The door, please?" she called through the screen. "I emptied an old recipe box so we can start our Memory Box," she said, handing me a treasure chest a pirate would love. "Now I'll leave my men alone."

My fingers traced the designs carved in the smooth, shiny wood.

"I gave that to your grandmother on our wedding day," was all Gramps said. Then we sat in the dark and watched the fireflies dart past the porch. Maybe Gramps was already searching his mind for memories to put in the box. He never said.

But for the rest of my vacation, we remembered, Gramps and Gram and me. We especially remembered when we were fishing. "Thoughts come faster when bobbers are jumping," Gram said as she wrote our memories on paper scarps.

"How about the time I climbed the water tower?" I asked Gramps. "Mom said no, but you turned your back so I could make it to the top."

"You nearly fell off, as I recall." He scratched the whiskers that appeared on his face for the first summer ever. I wondered about those whiskers. Didn't Gramps tell me once how much Gram hated it when he didn't shave?

"How about the time I laid my freshly picked blueberries on the porch to sun-dry?" Gram remembered. "Zach came in from his swim and squished a path right through those juicy berries."

"Looked like an old blue rug to me," I said, remembering how Gram's face had turned red and my feet had turned blue at the same time.

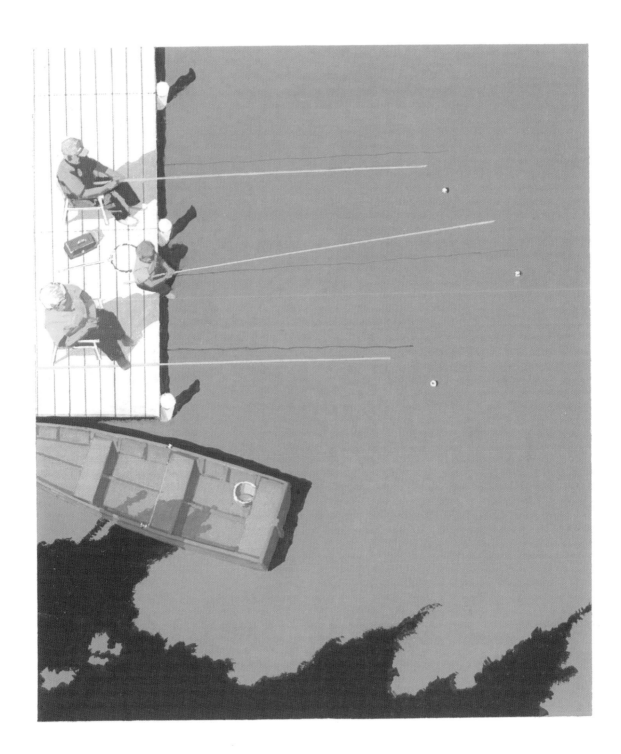

It was Gramps's job to add photos and souvenirs to the Memory Box. He found a picture of my second birthday party when I had taken a bite off the top of the cake. There was a shot of Gram in her wedding dress with flowers in her hair and one of Dad in his football uniform when he still had hair. Another was of Gramps and Mom the day he had taught her to ride a bike. She had ridden it, too. Right over his foot!

We added other important stuff, like my first soccer medal and Gram's chocolate-chip cookie recipe.

We added new memories, too.

We wrote about the morning the three of us rolled green apples down the hill for a herd of deer that rested in the long grass.

And the time we watched a raccoon bandit watch *us* as she ate a trayful of cookies that Gram had set to cool on the picnic table.

And a picture of the trophy walleye I caught the morning we put the boat on the lake before the sun even got up.

As the days passed, I noticed something different about Gramps. A major small change, if you know what I mean. One afternoon I saw him sitting in the swing that hung between two giant pines. I headed on over. But I stopped when I heard him talking to somebody else. Gramps was telling Francie how to reel in a northern pike that was fighting her hook. He was talking to her as if she were right there. But nobody was. Especially not Francie—she's my mom.

And one afternoon we hiked to find nature stuff I could take back to school. Gramps wandered off the trail into a poison ivy patch as if he didn't even see it. I yelled until he stopped, but he wouldn't come back. I had to go get him and take him by the hand. That day it seemed like his body walked with me, but his thoughts strolled somewhere else.

None of it made sense until the morning Gram shook me awake.

"Get dressed, Zach. Help me find Gramps. He's been gone too long."

"Probably just fishing." I stared at Gram as if she were a crazy lady.

"But he forgot his shoes." She looked back at me as if I were the crazy one. "Check the shed. Whistle if you find him first."

I ran toward the lake, even faster when I saw the shed door swinging. But Gramps wasn't inside.

Outside again, I stopped to listen, the way hunters do. I thought I heard noises out back, so I circled the woods around the shed. When I found Gramps, I whistled loud. He was sitting on the ground like a scout in front of a campfire. His feet were bare, and one was bleeding.

"Forgot my shoes." He tried to hide his face. It was shiny with tears.

Gram moved the fastest I'd ever seen. She sat on the ground beside Gramps while I ran back for his slippers. We helped him back to the house. Led him, if you want to know the truth. While we bandaged his foot and made him lie down on his bed, Gramps was quiet. We waited until the snoring began before Gram and I tiptoed out of the room.

"Remember that first Memory Box night?" Gram asked. She sat in the kitchen. "Gramps was trying to tell you about Alzheimer's disease…when the body stays but the mind leaves."

She stared off, and I just waited until she looked at me again.

"The mind doesn't go all at once, or all the time, but it never comes back quite the same way. When Dr. Johnson suggested Gramps might have Alzheimer's, it explained so many things about this past year—Gramps forgetting to shave, his talking to me like we were kids again, his getting lost on trails he'd hiked for years."

I thought about the poison ivy and Francie's fishing lesson.

"It scares Gramps, knowing he'll forget. That's why the Memory Box is so important."

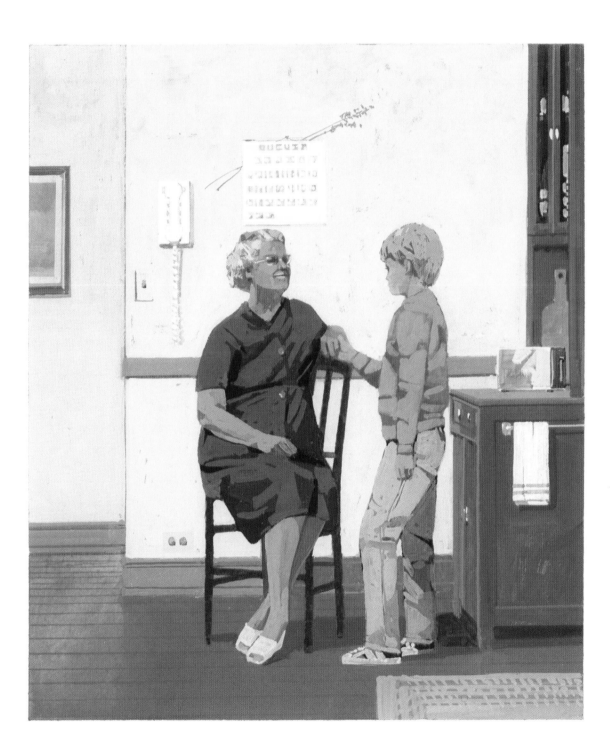

When Gramps woke up, he called me. I stood at his bedroom door. He sat on the bed.

"Did Gram tell you about this useless old man? And how he needs to find a home for special things like this?" He handed me the old fishing knife from the shed. "I forgot the sheath, so I went back…and got lost."

"Thanks," I whispered, holding the knife the way Gramps had taught me. My own, very first knife. I'd always wanted one. This one. But now it didn't seem so important.

"Your Mom's going to hurt," Gramps said. "When it gets bad, bring out our Memory Box. Show her what I remember."

I hugged Gramps. We both felt better.

The rest of my vacation bolted like a fawn when you try to sneak too close. The day Dad and Mom came to take me back for school, we had such a great barbecue that we decided it should be part of the Memory Box. I could tell Dad already knew about Gramps because he shot a zillion photos of Gramps and Gram.

When it was time to leave, Gramps squeezed me hard.

Gram squeezed me soft. "Add things to the Memory Box you want Gramps to remember," she whispered as she handed it to me. "And bring it with you next summer. "We'll need it, you and I."

I waved as our car drove away—away from the best and worst summer ever. This time Gramps and Gram had taken care of me. Next summer, Gram and I would take care of Gramps. And the summers after that…well, we'd figure out something.

As the car hit the top of the hill, I watched Gramps
slowly disappear into the horizon.
And I hugged my Memory Box.